For Liam

RACE TO THE FINISH!
A RED FOX BOOK 978 0 099 49517 8

First published in Great Britain by Hutchinson,
an imprint of Random House Children's Publishers UK
A Random House Group Company

Hutchinson edition published as *Little Red Train's Race to the Finish* 2006
Red Fox edition published 2009

13

Red Fox Books are published by Random House Children's Publishers UK,
61–63 Uxbridge Road, London W5 5SA

www.**randomhousechildrens**.co.uk

Addresses for companies within The Random House Group Limited can be found at:
www.randomhouse.co.uk/offices.htm

THE RANDOM HOUSE GROUP Limited Reg. No. 954009

A CIP catalogue record for this book is available from the British Library.

Printed in China

RACE TO THE FINISH!

RACE TO THE FINISH!

Benedict Blathwayt

RED FOX

Duffy Driver and Jack the guard were fed up.

"Those Swish Trains," said Jack. "They're taking over! And now they want the route to Barnacle Bay."

"The Little Red Train will have nothing to do!" said Duffy.

The Swish Train drivers just laughed at Duffy and Jack.

"Your train is old and slow," they said.

"Everybody loves the Little Red Train," said Duffy. "It's not *that* slow!"

"Prove it then!" sneered the drivers. "We'll race you to Barnacle Bay. Whoever wins the race, wins the route."

Duffy and Jack got ready for the big race.
  "We've got to win by miles," whispered the Swish driver,
"so no one will want to use the Little Red Train ever again."

Down went the flag . . .
They were off!
Puff chuff, puff chuff
went the Little Red Train.

Sweeeeeeeeeesh! went the Swish Train as it sped past and out of sight.
    "Oh, rust and dust!" said Duffy.

But worse was to come . . .

At the very first hill, the Little Red
Train's wheels began to spin.

"There's oil on the tracks," said Duffy.
"I wonder how it got there."

The passengers pushed the Little Red Train over the top of the hill.

"We can still catch up!"
yelled Jack.
    But worse was to come . . .

Sheep on the line!

Duffy put on the brakes with a *screeeeech* and they stopped just in time.

"I wonder who left the gate open," said Duffy.

At the next station the Swish Train driver had stopped
for a cup of tea. He seemed very surprised indeed to
see the Little Red Train.

Duffy steamed past without slowing down.

Chuff chuff chuffitty chuff

But soon enough the Swish Train passed them again and
disappeared into the distance with a great *swoooooooosh!*
    "Oh, coke and clinker!" said Duffy.
    But worse was to come . . .

Suddenly the Little Red Train went off in the wrong direction.

"Someone's switched the points," said Duffy. "But who?"

Duffy put on the brakes and started to go back.

"Whoa!" said Jack. "Keep going! This is the *old* way to Barnacle Bay. It will lead back on to the main line and straight to the finish."

So the Little Red Train kept going.
"Hold on tight!" shouted Duffy.

"There hasn't been a train along here for years," said Duffy.
"Don't slow down!" Jack shouted from his van.

When they reached the main line again, Jack switched the points. Now the Little Red Train was back on the right track.

"There's Barnacle Bay!"
cried Duffy.
 "And here comes the
Swish Train!" yelled Jack.

The roar of the Swish Train grew louder and louder.
The Little Red Train went faster and faster . . .
Clicketty clack, clicketty clack, clicketty clicketty clicketty clack!

But the Swish Train could not catch up and the Little Red
Train won the race!

"Hooray!" shouted the passengers.

"Hooray!" shouted Duffy and Jack.

Whoooooossssssssh went the steam from the Little Red Train.

When the celebrations were over, Duffy,
Jack and the Little Red Train headed home.
"I think Barnacle Bay is my favourite
place in the world," said Jack.
"Me too," said Duffy. And he blew the
Little Red Train's whistle, long and loud.
Whooooo . . . ooooooooo . . . eeeeeeeeeeeeeee!

More exciting stories to enjoy!

Picture Story Books

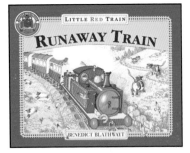

(also available as a Story Book and CD)

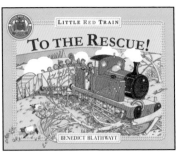

(also available as a Story Book and CD)

(also available as a Story Book and CD)

(also available as a Story Book and CD)

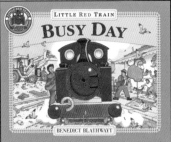

(also available as a Story Book and CD)

Gift Books

Stop That Train! – A Pop-Through-the-Slot Book

Little Red Train Adventure Playset

The Runaway Train Pop-up Book

The Runaway Train Sticker Frieze

The Little Red Train Gift Collection

The Runaway Train Book and DVD